Spread the Smile

Written by Debra Webster & Jackie Wilson
Illustrated by Debra Webster

First published in 2021 by Fuzzy Flamingo
www.fuzzyflamingo.co.uk

© 2021 Debra Webster and Jackie Wilson
Illustrations © 2021 Debra Webster

ISBN: 978-1-8384388-8-3

Design by Jen Parker, Fuzzy Flamingo
www.fuzzyflamingo.co.uk

*This book is dedicated with love to our children and greatest teachers
Katie, Adam, Katherine, Natalie and Chloe*

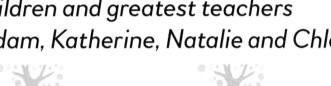

Jane and Jack were really good friends,
And went outside to play.
They loved to have adventures
On a bright and sunny day.

Jack ran right across the fields,
Followed by his friend Jane,
But they hadn't gone so very far
When it began to rain.

The grass got slippery and quite soggy,
So they slowed their pace a bit.
When the reached the stream it got quite boggy,
And they looked for a place to sit.

It was then Jane realised her mistake
And she began to sob
Because her favourite welly boot
Was stuck right in the bog.

Jack tried to calm her down a bit
And told her she'd be fine,
But it really wasn't working much
... along came Bunny,
just in time.

"Take three quick breaths, sniff, sniff, sniff...
Then one out really slowly..."
The charming Bunny said,
"I call it Bunny breathing."

Jane and Jack both tried it out,
And calmed down just like that.
"That's really clever, a super trick!"
Laughed Jane and her best friend Jack.

Out popped the boot with Bunny's help
And they jumped excitedly.
"You see there is a little trick,
Which makes you feel quite happy."

"Show us more please, this is fun!"
Said Jack and Jane together,
So they ran into the meadow,
Among flowers, grass and heather.

Then Jack shouted, "Aargh a bee!"
And flapped his arms around.
Bunny smiled and softly said,
"Just listen to that sound."

The bee continued collecting pollen
And gave a happy hummmmm.
The sound was lovely, soft and calming,
So they joined in with the hum.

"You see they really are not scary
And that sound can help a lot.
But before we rush off anywhere,
I almost quite forgot.

Let's take 5 and stop a while
And think what to do next."

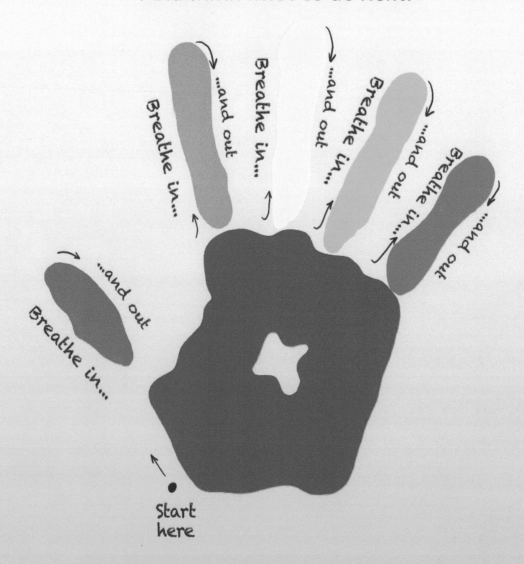

Breathe in...
...and out
Breathe in...
...and out
Breathe in...
...and out
Breathe in...
...and out
Breathe in...
...and out

Start
here

They breathed and traced their fingers
And enjoyed the little rest.

He lay down on the soft green grass,
The children copied too.
They watched the last few rain clouds,
Moving slowly out of view.

If ever you're unhappy,
Feeling scared or sad or mad,
You can blow the feeling to a cloud,
So you don't feel so bad.

The feelings land upon the clouds
And drift away from you.
Watch them float across the sky,
Just breathe and blow them through.

Then Bunny said, "I've got to go,
I've got lots to do."
"We've learned so much!" said Jack and Jane,
"We really do thank you."

"I know," said Jack,
"let's climb a tree."
And Jack and Jane
raced off.
They scrambled
through the branches,
Almost to the top.

From there the children looked around
And saw their family by the gate.
Their hearts were filled with happiness
And they really couldn't wait.

"Let's tell them all the things we've learned
With Bunny on our journey!"
They raced back down the tree again
And hurried to their family.

"Look at all of Bunny's tools. They can help you to Feel calm, relaxed and happy. Let us show you what to do."

"We'd really like to teach you,
So you can use it too.
And we can help each other
When we're feeling blue."

Its's always good to talk things through
And share your feelings too.
And don't forget to spread the smile,
That smile will work for you.

Useful Links

Here are some great additional resources to support children's emotional development :

www.emotionstoolkit.com

www.empowereducation.co.uk

www.debsta.com

www.positivelyempoweredkids.co.uk

www.positivepants.co.uk

www.wellbeingforkidsuk.com

www.skylark-consulting.co.uk

www.jwbridgethegap.com

www.gittewintergraugaard.dk

www.ollieandhissuperpowers.com

www.insideoutosyp.co.uk

www.mineconkbayir.co.uk

We are supported by these childcare settings, who recognise the importance of embedding self-regulation in the early years:

www.thrivechildcare.com
www.littledarlingchildcare.co.uk
www.children1stdaynurseries.com

Check out our amazing Emotions Toolkit® Spread the Smile Activity Book. This book complements the story, sharing how to do all of the tools in Bunny's toolkit along with activities to develop children's emotional literacy and some fantastic top tips for the grown ups ☺

Visit: www.emotionstoolkit.com

About the Authors

Jackie and Debra met in 2018 and the Emotions Toolkit® came to life. It has been an exciting collaboration as they are both passionate about preventing the mental health problems that so many people face without the self-regulation tools to manage their emotions more easily.

Jackie is a Youth Empowerment Coach, Keynote Speaker, Mindfulness Teacher and alongside the Emotions Toolkit®, she is also founder of Empower Education and co-founder of Positively Empowered Kids CIC.

Debra is a qualified teacher, specialising in the early years, with over 20 years' experience. Alongside the Emotions Toolkit®, she is a Children's Empowerment Mentor, and founder of Debsta Productions working as an artist and illustrator.

They both provide programmes, workshops and 1-1 sessions suitable for children, teens, parents and educators to support self-regulation and resilience.

We hope you love the book as much as we do,
Big smiles
Jackie & Debs